Kiddie Kindness
and the Good News

Daniel Holdsworth
Illustrated by Andy Robb

Concordia Publishing House

This parable about kindness is part of a series that teaches about the Fruit of the Spirit. God showed His grace and kindness to us by sending Jesus to die for our sins and rise again. The Holy Spirit helps us show kindness to others.

It was a day just like any other day in Heartland, except for one thing. Today was the day Kiddie Kindness was going to get her new bike. She had been looking forward to this day for a long time and at last it had come. Her shiny, red mountain bike would be perfect for all those mountains she had to face.

Kiddie Kindness had the special job of delivering the Good News to everyone in Heartland. The Good News was Heartland's very own newspaper. It often appeared at surprising times, so Kiddie Kindness always needed to be ready, just in case. Late one afternoon, the Good News arrived. Kiddie Kindness got her newspaper bag ready and set off on her shiny, red mountain bike to deliver the newspapers.

Kindness did not know that the very first mountain she would face was, in fact, a Dirty Potato called Envy.

"Stop, Kiddie Kindness!" shouted Envy.
"If you're so kind you'll give me your new bike."

As Envy dived forward to grab the shiny, red mountain
bike, his foot got caught on a rock. He tripped and fell
headfirst into a mud puddle.

"I'm sorry," called Kindness as she cycled off down the hill, "but I need my bike to deliver the Good News. I don't want to be late."

Envy was not a happy Dirty Potato. In fact, not being able to have something he wanted was what made Envy a very unhappy Dirty Potato.

"I know what I'll do," muttered Envy to himself. "I'll go and tell my friend, Strife. He'll be sure to stir up trouble for Kiddie Kindness." By the time Envy had finished telling him about the shiny, red mountain bike, Strife was itching to go and do something about it.

The next day, the Good News arrived early and Kiddie Kindness started to make her deliveries. The first stop was Mailman Faithfulness.

As Kindness turned the corner, she heard a loud bang followed by another loud bang. "Oh no," said Kiddie Kindness. "My tires are going flat. How in Heartland did that happen?"

"Easy," said a familiar voice. It was Strife who had been hiding in the bushes. In his hand he was holding a box of tacks.

"Give me your bike," growled Envy who had been hiding in the bushes as well. "I've told you, I need this bike for my job," said Kiddie Kindness.

"Well, you won't be going very far today," chuckled Strife. Envy and Strife found this very funny and the two of them laughed so hard they fell over and landed on the tacks. "Ouch, ouch!" they yelped as they hobbled off.

Mailman Faithfulness came outside to see what all the
commotion was about. He saw that Kindness was in
trouble. He went back to his house and returned with a
tire repair kit. "We'll have those tires fixed in no time,"
said Faithfulness.

In no time at all, Kindness was ready to continue her deliveries of the Good News.

"Thanks, Mailman Faithfulness," called Kiddie Kindness as she sped off as quickly as she could, hoping to make up for lost time. Nobody saw much of Envy and Strife for the next few days. They were both too busy nursing their wounds.

A week later, Kiddie Kindness ran into Doctor Gentleness on her last stop. Suddenly, as if from nowhere, a large log rolled in front of her.

Kindness had no time to stop and the front wheel of her bike hit the log. She flew over the handlebars and landed on the grass with a bump.

Dazed and hurting, Kiddie Kindness looked up. She saw Envy and Strife hiding in the bushes and looking very pleased with what they had done.

"That'll teach you to not give me your bike," called Envy as they raced down the lane.

Gentleness helped Kindness, making sure she was all right. "First I'll mend your cuts and bruises," said Doctor Gentleness, "and then we'll mend your bike."

As the sun was setting, Kiddie Kindness headed home on her mended mountain bike.

"I wonder if Envy and Strife will ever stop making trouble," sighed Kiddie Kindness with tears in her eyes. "I do hope they will."

The very next day, Envy and Strife were up to their old tricks, but this time Kindness was ready for them. As she started to deliver the Good News she met Sergeant Self-Control.

"I hear your bike has been through a lot lately. Is that right?" he asked. "Yes, but it wasn't this bike," said Kiddie Kindness. She was riding a shiny, blue mountain bike. "This bike is not mine. This bike is for someone else."

Kindness finished explaining about the new, blue bike. Out from the bushes jumped Envy and Strife. They didn't see Sergeant Self-Control. Before they knew what happened, he grabbed both of them so they couldn't wriggle away.

"Well, well, look what I've caught," smiled the Sergeant.

"I think Kiddie Kindness has something to do for you," said Sergeant Self-Control.

Kiddie Kindness looked at the Dirty Potatoes and smiled. "I certainly do!" she said. "I really am sorry I couldn't give you my shiny, red mountain bike, but I needed it to finish my job of delivering the Good News."

"And the good news today, Envy, is that this new bike is for you." Envy didn't know what to say. He was so overcome by kindness he began to cry.

So did Strife, but that was only because he knew that there was no more work for him to do in Heartland.

To Remember: The good news of Jesus' death and resurrection overcomes envy and strife as the Holy Spirit helps us share God's kindness with others.

"[God] expressed His kindness to us in Christ Jesus."
Ephesians 2:7